The Phantom's Last Voyage

by Valerie Thame

Series Editors: Steve Barlow and Steve Skidmore

Published by Heinemann Educational Publishers
Halley Court, Jordan Hill, Oxford OX2 8EJ
A division of Reed Educational and Professional Publishing Ltd

OXFORD MELBOURNE AUCKLAND
JOHANNESBURG BLANTYRE GABORONE
IBADAN PORTSMOUTH NH (USA) CHICAGO

05 04 03 02 01
10 9 8 7 6 5 4 3 2 1
ISBN 0 435 21509 4

Illustrations by Andrew Skilleter
Cover design by Shireen Nathoo Design
Cover artwork by Paul Young
Designed by Artistix, Thame, Oxon
Printed and bound in Great Britain by Athenaeum Press Ltd

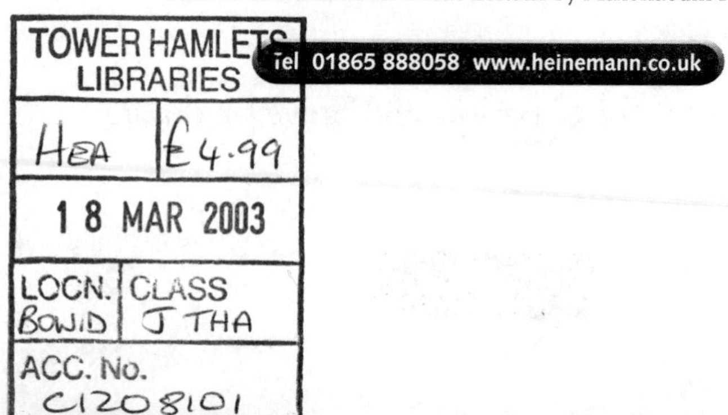

Contents

Prologue

THE CORNISH NEWS

LOCAL BOY DROWNED

Tragic Death of Father and Son

A sixteen-year-old boy fell into the sea last Monday. He was out fishing with his father. When their fishing boat, *The Phantom*, did not return, the coast-guards were called out. The boat was found and the father saved.

Mr Josh Tully, known as 'Tully', had been in the sea for over three hours, looking for his missing son. A coastguard said, 'The weather was very bad at the time. The boy must have drowned.'

Sadly, Tully did not recover from the shock of losing his son. He died the next day. Tully had no other family. His boat and cottage will be sold. His son's body has still not been found.

CHAPTER 1

Dave woke up on the floor. His heart was pounding loudly. Something had woken him up. But what? Then he remembered his dream.

He had dreamed he was drowning. He was in the sea, fighting for his life. The waves were huge and kept pushing him under. When he cried out, his mouth filled with salt water. He was scared. He thought he was going to die.

Dave shivered. The dream had been so real. He sat up and looked at his watch. It was midnight. But why was he on the floor?

He must have fallen out of bed. But the dream had felt so real. He had never done that before. And where was he? This was not his room.

Then he remembered where he was. It was his first night at the holiday cottage in Cornwall.

The cottage was called *Tully's*. It stood high on the cliffs above the sea. *Tully's* was very old and had been empty for years.

Dave thought it was grim, but his parents had plans to 'do it up' as a holiday home.

Dave climbed back into bed and tried to forget his dream. He turned to the wall and pulled the duvet over his head.

He did not see the damp footprints that suddenly appeared on the floorboards by his bed. He did not hear the gentle voice that called his name.

'Dave? Davey? Is that you, lad?'

CHAPTER 2

When Dave woke up the following morning, the sun was shining. Everything looked good. Even the old cottage looked better than it had yesterday.

'I'm going for a walk,' said Dave, after breakfast.

'Where to?' said his mother.

She was already busy clearing out the kitchen cupboards.

'Nowhere. Just to look around,' said Dave.

'There's plenty of work to be done here,' said his father. 'Floors to scrub. Walls to wash. Painting to do. How about it?'

'No thanks!' said Dave. 'It wasn't my idea to buy this old dump. I can think of better things to do with my holiday.'

He got out as quickly as possible. Painting an old cottage was not his idea of fun. If it had been anywhere else but Cornwall, Dave would not have come. He loved the sea and boats. His dream was to have a boat of his own some day.

The path outside the cottage led right down to the sea. Dave walked slowly along the path. The tide was out. The harbour was empty except for one or two small boats. A man was painting a rowing boat and Dave stopped to watch. Now that sort of painting was OK. He would enjoy working on a boat.

'Hello!' said a voice behind him.

He turned to face a girl with dark, curly hair and a friendly smile. He guessed she was about fifteen, a bit younger than he was.

'Hi!' said Dave.

'Are you on holiday?' said the girl.

Dave shrugged. 'Yeah, sort of.'

'My name's Katy. My mum runs the teashop over there.' She pointed to a café on the other side of the harbour. 'So, what's *your* name, then?' she said.

'Dave.'

'How long are you here for, Dave?'

'Three weeks. My parents have bought Tully's cottage, as a holiday home.'

Katy looked surprised. 'Tully's cottage? I didn't think anybody would ever buy that place. Of course, we get a few grockles looking round every summer.'

'Grockles? What are grockles?'

'Sorry, that's our word for visitors. People who don't live here. Not local.'

'Like me, you mean?' said Dave.

Katy blushed. 'Well, yes.'

'But there must be lots of holiday homes round here,' said Dave.

'Yes, there are. But *Tully's* is different.'

'You can say that again. It's a dump,' said Dave. 'It's falling down. But my parents are into DIY – big time. Not me though. I'm into boats.'

'Have you got a boat?' asked Katy.

'No, but I'd like one.'

'You take care,' said Katy. 'The sea round here can be very dangerous. There are strong tides and lots of hidden rocks under the cliffs.'

'I know that. I'm not a kid, you know,' said Dave.

'Sorry. Only trying to be helpful.'

Dave walked on down the path.

Katy went with him.

'They say that cottage still belongs to Tully,' she said.

'Do they? Well, they're wrong,' said Dave. 'Who was he anyway?'

'Just a fisherman.'

'So what happened? Did he sell up? Move away?' asked Dave.

'No, he died after an accident at sea.'

'Well, he can't own the cottage if he's dead, can he?'

'I didn't say he owned it,' said Katy. 'I said it still belonged to him. Do you know what I mean?'

'No, I don't. You said he died at sea.'

'I didn't! I said there was an accident at sea. He died the next day, at home, in his big, old bed.'

'Yeah, and it's still there,' said Dave. 'I have to sleep in it.'

'You've slept in Tully's bed?'

'Yep.'

'Spooky,' said Katy.

CHAPTER 3

They walked down to the harbour together. Katy did most of the talking, while Dave listened. She told him that her mum and dad were divorced. Her mum ran the *Harbour Café* and she helped after school.

'And I go clubbing most Saturday nights, but I don't have a steady boyfriend,' she added.

'Right,' said Dave.

No boyfriend? Was she trying to tell him something? Did this mean she fancied him?

Katy stopped outside the café.

'Can I buy you a drink?' she said.

'Thanks,' said Dave.

He smiled. So she *did* fancy him. Well, that was OK, but he was only here for three weeks.

They sat at a table by the window. 'Since I'm living in Tully's cottage, I'd like to know more about him,' said Dave.

'Like what?'

'You tell me. Was he old? Was he young? How did he die? And what's so "spooky" about me sleeping in his bed?'

'Well, it's all very odd,' said Katy.

Dave grinned. He had a feeling that Katy was enjoying this.

'Like I said, Tully was a fisherman. He had one son who was about your age when the accident happened. Fifteen or sixteen?'

'Right.' Dave nodded.

'Tully and his son were out fishing. There was a bad storm and the son fell overboard. Tully jumped in the sea to save him, but he couldn't see him anywhere. He swam around for hours, looking for him. He nearly drowned too. By the time Tully was found, he was nearly out of his mind. He died the next day in his bed. The bed you sleep in.'

'And that's the spooky bit, is it?' said Dave.

'That's part of it. But they also say that, before he died, Tully made a vow to come back and find his son. No matter what. No matter how.'

Dave smiled. 'And has he?'

'Well, that's the point,' said Katy. 'They say Tully's ghost is still looking for his son.'

'Yeah? Well, I don't believe in ghosts. It's a load of old rubbish.'

Katy looked hurt. She stood up.

'Well, *you're* the one asking questions. If you don't like the answers – too bad! Anyway, I've got to go. I'm meant to be working.'

'OK. See you later,' said Dave.

'Maybe,' said Katy.

CHAPTER 4

Dave left the café and went for a walk along the cliffs. He knew he had upset Katy, but he wasn't sure why.

He spent the morning sitting on the cliffs, watching the sea and the boats. He had nothing to do and was in no hurry to go home.

When he got back to the cottage, the downstairs rooms were empty. His parents had been busy.

'I'm home!' he shouted.

'We're upstairs. Clearing out our bedroom,' shouted his mother.

Dave went out to the backyard. It was full of furniture from the cottage. Old chairs, tables and other bits of rubbish. He noticed a picture that he liked. It was of a boat called *The Phantom*. He took it upstairs to his room.

'Is that you, Dave?' called his father. 'Give us a hand with this wardrobe, will you? It's stuck – we can't get out of the bedroom!'

Dave helped his father to move the

wardrobe. After that, his mum got him scrubbing floorboards. By the time he went to bed that night, he was worn out.

He fell asleep straight away, but he had another nightmare. He was on a boat in a storm. The boat pitched and tossed, as it drifted towards the rocks. Dave tried to steer it away from the cliffs, but the wheel would not turn.

The boat was flung into the air. Up and down. Up and down. Dave was feeling seasick. Then, a giant wave tossed the boat onto the rocks.

Dave woke up in a panic. The dream had been so real. His heart was thumping and he was sweating. He lay in bed, trying to relax. The cottage was still and silent.

Then he heard a sound that gave him goose pimples.

'Dave? Davey?'

It was just a whisper, but it was close by. Dave's heart beat even faster. He lay in the darkness, his eyes searching the shadows. But he saw and heard nothing more. He did not see the man who stood beside his bed. The man with wet boots. But he knew he was there.

CHAPTER 5

The next morning Dave was still thinking about the voice in the night. He had to talk to Katy.

He went straight down to the café. Katy was busy laying the tables.

'Hi!' said Dave. 'Look, I'm sorry if I upset you. Me and my big mouth!'

'Yes,' said Katy. She did not look too pleased.

'Well, I'm sorry. I need to ask you more about Tully.'

'I've told you all I know,' said Katy. 'Didn't you say it was all rubbish?'

'Yes, but something's happened.'

Katy's eyes lit up. 'You've seen him, haven't you? You've seen Tully's ghost.'

'No, not really,' said Dave, 'but I had a bad dream last night. When I woke up, I just knew somebody, or something, was in my room.'

'But you didn't see anything?'

Dave shook his head. 'No, but I thought I heard something.'

'Like what?' Katy was interested now.

'A voice.'

'A voice? Now that *is* spooky!' said Katy. 'Do you think it was Tully?'

'Maybe. But if his son drowned at sea, why would he come back to the house to look for him?'

'Well, he thinks his son is a ghost too,' said Katy. 'They're both dead. So, he'd look at home first, wouldn't he?'

'I hadn't thought of that,' said Dave. 'By the way, where is Tully's boat now?'

Katy pointed through the café windows. 'It's out there on the harbour wall. But it's a wreck. Tully had no family and nobody else wanted it.'

'I'd like to look at it,' said Dave.

'You can, but it's not safe. We've had a few accidents out there.'

Dave smiled. 'I'll be OK. I can look after myself. Do you want to come?'

'I can't. I've got to go to the cash-and-carry with Mum to get some stuff for the café. I'll be back about four o'clock.'

'OK, I'll see you then,' said Dave.

But he could not wait. As soon as he left the café, he went to see Tully's boat. Katy was right. It was a wreck. He could just read the name, painted on the side. *The Phantom!* It was the boat in his picture.

Dave climbed onto the deck of *The Phantom*. It didn't look much like the picture now. The wood was rotting away. Well, if nobody wanted it, he would take it on. Dave was sure he could make it seaworthy again. He tried to imagine the boat as it used to be. The wood polished and the paint shiny. It would take a lot of hard work, but he would not mind.

Dave did not notice the storm clouds

gathering. Suddenly, it was raining. In seconds, Dave was soaked. It was no good trying to run back to the café. It was too far away. He tried to open the cabin door, but it was stuck. Thunder rumbled in the sky and the rain came down even harder.

A strong wind shook the old wreck. It did not feel safe. Dave knew he had to get off the boat and find shelter. He scrambled across the deck. The wind pushed him back. He tripped and fell. He tried to grab something, but there was nothing to hold on to. Unable to stop himself falling, Dave crashed into the cabin. He shut his eyes. That was the last thing he remembered.

CHAPTER 6

When the storm was over, Tully's boat had gone from the harbour. Everybody thought it must have been washed out to sea. But what had happened to Dave? He had gone too. He did not keep his date with Katy and he did not go home that night.

His worried parents called the police. A huge search began and everybody joined in. They searched the cliffs, the caves and the beaches. The search was shown on television and was in all the papers. Nobody knew what had happened to the boy from Tully's cottage.

Katy thought she knew. She was sure Tully's ghost had mistaken Dave for his son. If only she had told Dave that he had the same name as the boy who had drowned. But Dave would have laughed at her. And now, he had had an accident on the old wreck. Katy knew he was dead.

A week later, her worst fears were realised. A body was washed up a mile down the coast.

CHAPTER 7

When Dave opened his eyes, he was surprised to find he was inside the boat's cabin. It was warm and dry. He looked down at his clothes. They were dry too. A man stood at the wheel. He had his back to Dave.

'I knew you'd come, Davey lad,' said the man. 'I've been waiting for you. See? I've got *The Phantom* all ship-shape and ready to go.'

Then Dave noticed the boat was moving. He stood up. They were still in the harbour, but it had stopped raining.

The sun was out and the sea was calm.

The man put a gentle hand on Dave's shoulder.

'She's a lovely boat, isn't she, Dave?'

Dave nodded. He was puzzled. How did this man know his name? He tried to remember what had happened and how he got here. But his mind was a total blank. He had no memory at all.

'She's yours now, Davey,' said the man. 'I always meant her to be.'

Suddenly, Dave's mind cleared. He was going fishing, wasn't he? And he'd just been given his own boat.

'Mine? That's great!' he said.

The man smiled. 'We'll have some fun together, you and me. Why don't you take

The Phantom out of the harbour?"

Dave had never steered a boat before. But it felt good, it felt right. *The Phantom* was no longer an old wreck. Her red and black paint shone in the sunlight. She looked as good as the day she was built.

With Dave at the wheel and Tully by his side, *The Phantom* glided out of the harbour towards the open sea.